D1210281

O TO BE A DRAGON

ALSO BY MARIANNE MOORE

Like a Bulwark
Predilections
Collected Poems

TRANSLATED BY MARIANNE MOORE

The Fables of La Fontaine

O TO BE A DRAGON

Marianne Moore

T H E   V I K I N G   P R E S S

New York · 1959

PS
3525
.O5616
O2
1959

COPYRIGHT © 1956, 1957, 1958, 1959 BY MARIANNE MOORE
COPYRIGHT © 1958 BY THE CURTIS PUBLISHING COMPANY

PUBLISHED IN 1959 BY THE VIKING PRESS, INC.
625 MADISON AVENUE, NEW YORK 22, N.Y.

PUBLISHED IN CANADA BY
THE MACMILLAN COMPANY OF CANADA LIMITED

SECOND PRINTING 1959
THIRD PRINTING 1959

Acknowledgment is made to the editors of the following publications in which certain of the pieces in this collection first appeared: "O to Be a Dragon," *Sequoia*, Autumn 1957. "Values in Use," *Partisan Review*, Autumn 1956. "Hometown Piece for Messrs. Alston and Reese," October 3, 1956, and "For February 14th," February 13, 1959, New York *Herald Tribune*. "Enough: Jamestown 1607–1957," *Virginia Quarterly Review*, Autumn 1957. "Melchior Vulpius," *Atlantic Monthly*, January 1958. "No better than 'a withered daffodil,' " *Art News*, March 1959. "In the Public Garden," *Ladies' Home Journal*, January 1959, with the title "Boston." "The Arctic Ox (or Goat)," September 13, 1958, "Saint Nicholas," December 27, 1958, "Combat Cultural," June 6, 1959, and "Leonardo da Vinci's," July 18, 1959, *The New Yorker*.

LIBRARY OF CONGRESS CATALOG CARD NUMBER: 59–12454

SET IN ALDINE BEMBO TYPES AND
PRINTED IN THE U.S.A. BY CLARKE & WAY

P   N   B

Contents

O TO BE A DRAGON

O to Be a Dragon

If I, like Solomon, . . .
could have my wish—

my wish . . . O to be a dragon,
a symbol of the power of Heaven—of silkworm
size or immense; at times invisible.
Felicitous phenomenon!

I May, I Might, I Must

If you will tell me why the fen
appears impassable, I then
will tell you why I think that I
can get across it if I try.

To a Chameleon

Hid by the august foliage and fruit
  of the grape-vine
  twine
    your anatomy
      round the pruned and polished stem,
      Chameleon.
      Fire laid upon
      an emerald as long as
    the Dark King's massy
  one,
could not snap the spectrum up for food
  as you have done.

A Jellyfish

Visible, invisible,
   a fluctuating charm
an amber-tinctured amethyst
   inhabits it, your arm
approaches and it opens
   and it closes; you had meant
to catch it and it quivers;
   you abandon your intent.

Values in Use

I attended school and I liked the place—
grass and little locust-leaf shadows like lace.

Writing was discussed. They said, "We create
values in the process of living, daren't await

their historic progress." Be abstract
and you'll wish you'd been specific; it's a fact.

What was I studying? Values in use,
"judged on their own ground." Am I still abstruse?

Walking along, a student said offhand,
"'Relevant' and 'plausible' were words I understand."

A pleasing statement, anonymous friend.
Certainly the means must not defeat the end.

Hometown Piece for Messrs. Alston and Reese

To the tune:
"Li'l baby, don't say a word: Mama goin' to buy you a mocking-bird.
Bird don't sing: Mama goin' to sell it and buy a brass ring."

"Millennium," yes; "pandemonium"!
Roy Campanella leaps high. Dodgerdom

crowned, had Johnny Podres on the mound.
Buzzie Bavasi and the Press gave ground;

the team slapped, mauled, and asked the Yankees' match,
"How did you feel when Sandy Amoros made the catch?"

"I said to myself"—pitcher for all innings—
"as I walked back to the mound I said, 'Everything's

getting better and better.'" (Zest, they've zest.
" 'Hope springs eternal in the Brooklyn breast.' "

And would the Dodger Band in 8, row 1, relax
if they saw the collector of income tax?

Ready with a tune if that should occur:
"Why Not Take All of Me—All of Me, Sir?")

Another series. Round-tripper Duke at bat,
"Four hundred feet from home-plate"; more like that.

A neat bunt, please; a cloud-breaker, a drive
like Jim Gilliam's great big one. Hope's alive.

Homered, flied out, fouled? Our "stylish stout"
so nimble Campanella will have him out.

A-squat in double-headers four hundred times a day,
he says that in a measure the pleasure is the pay:

catcher to pitcher, a nice easy throw
almost as if he'd just told it to go.

[14]

Willie Mays should be a Dodger. He should—
a lad for Roger Craig and Clem Labine to elude;

but you have an omen, pennant-winning Peewee,
on which we are looking superstitiously.

Ralph Branca has Preacher Roe's number; recall?
and there's Don Bessent; he can really fire the ball.

As for Gil Hodges, in custody of first—
"He'll do it by himself." Now a specialist versed

in an extension reach far into the box seats—
he lengthens up, he leans, and gloving the ball defeats

expectation by a whisker. The modest star,
irked by one misplay, is no hero by a hair;

in a strikeout slaughter when what could matter more,
he lines a homer to the signboard and has changed the score.

Then for his nineteenth season, a home run—
with four of six runs batted in—Carl Furillo's the big gun;

almost dehorned the foe—has fans dancing in delight.
Jake Pitler and his Playground "get a Night"—

Jake, that hearty man, made heartier by a harrier
who can bat as well as field—Don Demeter.

Shutting them out for nine innings—a hitter too—
Carl Erskine leaves Cimoli nothing to do.

Take off the goat-horns, Dodgers, that egret
which two very fine base-stealers can offset.

You've got plenty: Jackie Robinson
and Campy and big Newk, and Dodgerdom again
watching everything you do. You won last year.
                                        Come on.

Enough

Some in the Godspeed, the Susan C.,
others in the Discovery,

found their too earthly paradise.
Dazzled, the band, with grateful cries

clutched the soil; then worked upstream,
safer if landlocked, it would seem;

to pests and pestilence instead—
the living outnumbered by the dead.

Their namesake ships traverse the sky
as jets to Jamestown verify.

The same reward for best and worst
doomed communism, tried at first.

Three acres each, initiative,
six bushels paid back, they could live.

Captain Dale became kidnaper—
the master—lawless when the spur

was desperation, even though
his victim had let her victim go—

Captain John Smith. Poor Powhatan
had to make peace, embittered man.

Then teaching—insidious recourse—
enhanced Pocahontas and flowered of course

in marriage. John Rolfe fell in love
with her and she—in rank above

what she became—renounced her name
yet found her status not too tame.

[16]

The crested moss-rose casts a spell;
its bud of solid green, as well,

and the Old Pink Moss—with fragrant wings
imparting balsam scent that clings

where redbrown tanbark holds the sun,
resilient beyond comparison.

Not to begin with. No select
artlessly perfect French effect

mattered at first. (Small point to rhymes
for maddened men in starving-times.)

Tested until unnatural,
one became a cannibal.

Marriage, tobacco, and slavery,
initiated liberty

when the Deliverance brought seed
of that now controversial weed—

a blameless plant Red-Ridinghood.
Who, after all, knows what is good!

A museum of the mind "presents";
one can be stronger than events.

The victims of a search for gold
cast yellow soil into the hold.

With nothing but the feeble tower
to mark the site that did not flower,

could the most ardent have been sure
that they had done what would endure?

It was enough; it is enough
if present faith mend partial proof.

[17]

Melchior Vulpius
c. 1560—1615

a contrapuntalist—
                    composer of chorales
and wedding-hymns to Latin words
but best of all an anthem:
    "God be praised for conquering faith
    which feareth neither pain nor death."

We have to trust this art—
                    this mastery which none
can understand. Yet someone has
acquired it and is able to
    direct it. Mouse-skin-bellows'-breath
    expanding into rapture saith

"Hallelujah." Almost
                    utmost absolutist
and fugue-ist, Amen; slowly building
from miniature thunder,
    crescendos antidoting death—
    love's signature cementing faith.

No better than "a withered daffodil"

Ben Jonson said he was? "O I could still
Like melting snow upon some craggy hill,
    Drop, drop, drop, drop."

I too until I saw that French brocade
blaze green as though some lizard in the shade
    became exact—

set off by replicas of violet—
like Sidney, leaning in his striped jacket
    against a lime—

a work of art. And I too seemed to be
an insouciant rester by a tree—
    no daffodil.

In the Public Garden

Boston has a festival—
compositely for all—
and nearby, cupolas of learning
(crimson, blue, and gold) that
    have made education individual.

My first—an exceptional,
an almost scriptural—
taxi-driver to Cambridge from Back Bay said
as we went along, "They
    make some fine young men at Harvard." I recall

the summer when Faneuil Hall
had its weathervane with gold ball
and grasshopper, gilded again by
a -leafer and -jack
    till it glittered. Spring can be a miracle

there—a more than usual
bouquet of what is vernal—
"pear blossoms whiter than the clouds," pin-
oak leaves barely showing
    when other trees are making shade, besides small

fairy iris suitable
for Dulcinea del
Toboso; O yes, and snowdrops
in the snow, that smell like
    violets. Despite secular bustle,

let me enter King's Chapel
to hear them sing: "My work be praise while
others go and come. No more a stranger
or a guest but like a child
    at home." A chapel or a festival

means giving what is mutual,
even if irrational:
black sturgeon-eggs—a camel
from Hamadan, Iran;
   a jewel, or, what is more unusual,

   silence—after a word-waterfall of the banal—
   as unattainable
as freedom. And what is freedom for?
For "self-discipline," as our
   hardest-working citizen has said—a school;

   it is for "freedom to toil"
   with a feel for the tool.
Those in the trans-shipment camp must have
a skill. With hope of freedom hanging
   by a thread—some gather medicinal

   herbs which they can sell.
   Ineligible if they ail.
      Well?

There are those who will talk for an hour
without telling you why they have
   come. And I? This is no madrigal—

   no medieval gradual—
   but it is a grateful tale.
Without that radiance which poets
are supposed to have—
   unofficial, unprofessional, still one need not fail

   to wish poetry well
   where intellect is habitual—
glad that the Muses have a home and swans—
that legend can be factual;
   happy that Art, admired in general,
   is always actually personal.

The Arctic Ox (or Goat)

Derived from "Golden Fleece of the Arctic," by John J. Teal, Jr., who
rears musk oxen on his farm in Vermont, as set forth in the March 1958
issue of the Atlantic Monthly.

To wear the arctic fox
you have to kill it. Wear
    qiviut—the underwool of the arctic ox—
pulled off it like a sweater;
your coat is warm; your conscience, better.

I would like a suit of
qiviut, so light I did not
    know I had it on; and in the
course of time, another
since I had not had to murder

the "goat" that grew the fleece
that grew the first. The musk ox
    has no musk and it is not an ox—
illiterate epithet.
Bury your nose in one when wet.

It smells of water, nothing else,
and browses goatlike on
    hind legs. Its great distinction
is not egocentric scent
but that it is intelligent.

Chinchillas, otters, water rats,
and beavers keep us warm
    but think! a "musk ox" grows six pounds
of *qiviut*; the cashmere ram,
three ounces—that is all—of pashm.

Lying in an exposed spot,
basking in the blizzard,
    these ponderosos could dominate
the rare-hairs market in Kashan and yet
you could not have a choicer pet.

They join you as you work;
love jumping in and out of holes,
    play in water with the children,
learn fast, know their names,
will open gates and invent games.

While not incapable
of courtship, they may find its
    servitude and flutter, too much
like Procrustes' bed;
so some decide to stay unwed.

Camels are snobbish
and sheep, unintelligent;
    water buffaloes, neurasthenic—
even murderous.
Reindeer seem over-serious,

whereas these scarce *qivies*,
with golden fleece and winning ways,
    outstripping every fur-bearer—
there in Vermont quiet—
could demand Bold Ruler's diet:

Mountain Valley water,
dandelions, carrots, oats—
    encouraged as well—by bed
made fresh three times a day,
to roll and revel in the hay.

[23]

Insatiable for willow
leaves alone, our goatlike
    qivi-curvi-capricornus
sheds down ideal for a nest.
Song-birds find *qiviut* best.

Suppose you had a bag
of it; you could spin a pound
    into a twenty-four-or-five-
mile thread—one, forty-ply—
that will not shrink in any dye.

If you fear that you are
reading an advertisement,
    you are. If we can't be cordial
to these creatures' fleece,
I think that we deserve to freeze.

Saint Nicholas,

might I, if you can find it, be given
a chameleon with tail
that curls like a watch spring; and vertical
on the body—including the face—pale
tiger-stripes, about seven;
    (the melanin in the skin
    having been shaded from the sun by thin
        bars; the spinal dome
            beaded along the ridge
            as if it were platinum).

If you can find no striped chameleon,
might I have a dress or suit—
I guess you have heard of it—of *qiviut*?
and to wear with it, a taslon shirt, the drip-dry fruit
of research second to none;
    sewn, I hope, by Excello;
    as for buttons to keep down the collar-points, no.
        The shirt could be white—
            and be "worn before six,"
            either in daylight or at night.

But don't give me, if I can't have the dress,
a trip to Greenland, or grim
trip to the moon. The moon should come here. Let him
make the trip down, spread on my dark floor some dim
marvel, and if a success
    that I stoop to pick up and wear,
    I could ask nothing more. A thing yet more rare,
        though, and different,
            would be this: Hans von Marées'
            St. Hubert, kneeling with head bent,

form erect—in velvet, tense with restraint—
hand hanging down: the horse, free.
Not the original, of course. Give me
a postcard of the scene—huntsman and divinity—
    hunt-mad Hubert startled into a saint
    by a stag with a Figure entined.
        But why tell you what you must have divined?
        Saint Nicholas, O Santa Claus,
            would it not be the most
            prized gift that ever was!

For February 14th

Saint Valentine,
although late, would "some interested law
impelled to plod in the poem's cause"
be unwelcome with a line?

Might you have liked a stone
from a De Beers Consolidated Mine?
or badger-neat saber-thronged thistle
of Palestine—the leaves alone

down'd underneath,
worth a touch? or that mimosa-leafed vine
called an "alexander's armillary
sphere" fanning out in a wreath?

Or did the ark
preserve paradise-birds with jet-black plumes,
whose descendants might serve as presents?
But questioning is the mark
of a pest! Why think
only of animals in connection
with the ark or the wine Noah drank?
but that the ark did not sink.

Combat Cultural

One likes to see a laggard rook's high
speed at sunset to outfly the dark,
    or a mount well schooled for a medal—
front legs tucked under for the barrier,
    or team of leapers turned aerial.

I recall a documentary
of Cossacks: a visual fugue, a mist
    of swords that seemed to sever
heads from bodies—feet stepping as through
    harp-strings in a scherzo. However,

the quadrille of Old Russia for me:
with aimlessly drooping handkerchief
    snapped like the crack of a whip;
a deliriously spun-out-level
    frock-coat skirt, unswirled and a-droop

in remote promenade. Let me see . . .
Old Russia, did I say? Cold Russia
    this time: the prize bunnyhug
and platform-piece of experts in the
    trip-and-slug of wrestlers in a rug.

"Sacked" and ready for bed apparently—
with a jab, a kick, pinned to the wall,
    they work toward the edge and stick;
stagger off, and one is victim of a
    flipflop—leg having circled leg as thick.

[28]

Some art, because of high quality,
is unlikely to command high sales;
    yes, no doubt; but here, oh no;
not with the frozen North's Nan-ai-ans
    of the sack in their tight touch-and-go.

These battlers, dressed identically—
just one person—may, by seeming twins,
    point a moral, should I confess;
we must cement the parts of any
    objective symbolic of *sagesse*.

Leonardo da Vinci's

Saint Jerome and his lion
  in that hermitage
of walls half gone,
  share sanctuary for a sage—
joint-frame for impassioned ingenious
  Jerome versed in language—
and for a lion like one on the skin of which
  Hercules' club made no impression.

The beast, received as a guest,
  although some monks fled—
with its paw dressed
  that a desert thorn had made red—
stayed as guard of the monastery ass . . .
  which vanished, having fed
its guard, Jerome assumed. The guest then, like an ass,
  was made carry wood and did not resist,

but before long, recognized
  the ass and consigned
its terrorized
  thieves' whole camel-train to chagrined
Saint Jerome. The vindicated beast and
  saint somehow became twinned;
and now, since they behaved and also looked alike,
  their lionship seems officialized.

Pacific yet passionate—
  for if not both, how
could he be great?
  Jerome—reduced by what he'd been through—

with tapering waist no matter what he ate,
        left us the Vulgate. That in *Leo*,
the Nile's rise grew food checking famine,
        made lion's-mouth fountains appropriate,

        if not universally,
            at least not obscure.
        And here, though hardly a summary, astronomy—
            or pale paint—makes the golden pair
in Leonardo da Vinci's sketch, seem
            sun-dyed. Blaze on, picture,
saint, beast; and Lion Haile Selassie, with household
        lions as symbol of sovereignty.

Notes

(A title becomes line 1 when part of the first sentence.)

O to Be a Dragon (page 9)

Dragon: see secondary symbols, Volume II of *The Tao of Painting*, translated and edited by Mai-mai Sze, Bollingen Series 49 (New York: Pantheon, 1956).

Solomon's wish: "an understanding heart." I Kings 3:9.

Values in Use (page 13)

Philip Rahv, July 30, 1956, at the Harvard Summer School Conference on the Little Magazine, Alston Burr Hall, Cambridge, Massachusetts, gave as the standard for stories accepted by the *Partisan Review* "maturity, plausibility, and the relevance of the point of view expressed." "A work of art must be appraised on its own ground; we produce values in the process of living, do not await their historic progress in history." See *Partisan Review*, Fall 1956.

Hometown Piece for Messrs. Alston and Reese (page 14)

Messrs. Alston and Reese: Walter Alston, manager of the Brooklyn Dodgers; Harold (Peewee) Reese, captain of the Dodgers.

Line 1: *millennium.* "The millennium and pandemonium arrived at approximately the same time in the Brooklyn Dodgers' clubhouse at the Yankee Stadium yesterday." Roscoe McGowen, *New York Times*, October 5, 1955.

Line 2: *Roy Campanella.* Photograph: "Moment of Victory," *New York Times*, October 5, 1955.

Line 4: *Buzzie Bavasi.* "The policemen understood they were to let the players in first, but Brooklyn officials—Walter O'Malley, Arthur

[33]

(Red) Patterson, Buzzie Bavasi and Fresco Thompson—wanted the writers let in along with the players. This, they felt, was a different occasion and nobody should be barred." Roscoe McGowen, *New York Times*, October 5, 1955. E. J. Bavasi: Vice president of the Dodgers. William J. Briordy, "Campanella Gets Comeback Honors," *New York Times*, November 17, 1955.

Line 6: *when Sandy Amoros made the catch*. [Joe Collins to Johnny Podres]: " 'The secret of your success was the way you learned to control your change-up. . . .' 'I didn't use the change-up much in the seventh game of the world series,' said Johnny. 'The background was bad for it. So I used a fast ball that really had a hop on it.' . . .'Hey, Johnny,' said Joe, 'how did you feel when Amoros made that catch?' 'I walked back to the mound,' said Podres, 'and I kept saying to myself, "everything keeps getting better and better." ' " Arthur Daley, "Sports of the Times: Just Listening," *New York Times*, January 17, 1956.

Line 10: "*Hope springs eternal.*" Roscoe McGowen, "Brooklyn against Milwaukee," *New York Times*, July 31, 1956.

Line 11: *8, Row 1.* The Dodgers' Sym-Phoney Band sits in Section 8, Row 1, Seats 1 to 7, conducted by Lou Soriano (who rose by way of the snare-drum). "The Sym-Phoney is busy rehearsing a special tune for the Brooklyn income tax collector: It's "All of Me— Why Not Take All of Me?" William R. Conklin, "Maestro Soriano at Baton for 18th Brooklyn Season," *New York Times*, August 12, 1956.

Line 16: "*Four hundred feet . . .*" "Gilliam opened the game with a push bunt for a hit, and with one out Duke Snider belted the ball more than 400 feet to the base of the right-center-field wall. Gilliam came home but had to return to base when the ball bounced high into the stands for a ground-rule double." Roscoe McGowen, "Dodgers against Pittsburgh." Duke Snider "hit twenty-three homers in Ebbets Field for four successive years." John Drebinger, *New York Times*, October 1, 1956.

Line 19: "*stylish stout.*" [A catcher]: "He crouches in his wearying squat a couple of hundred times a day, twice that for double-headers."

[34]

Arthur Daley, "At Long Last," *New York Times Magazine*, July 9, 1956.

Line 29: *Preacher Roe's number. 28.* Venerated left-handed pitcher for Brooklyn who won 22 games in the season of 1951.

Line 42: *Jake* . . . "He's a Jake of All Trades—Jake Pitler, the Dodgers' first-base coach and cheer-leader." Joseph Sheehan, *New York Times*, September 16, 1956, "Dodgers Will Have a Night for Jake"—an honor accepted two years ago "with conditions": that contributions be for Beth-El Hospital Samuel Strausberg Wing. Keepsake for the "Night": a replica of the plaque in the Jake Pitler Pediatric Playroom (for underprivileged children).

Line 44: *Don Demeter.* Center fielder, a newcomer from Fort Worth, Texas. "Sandy Amoros whacked an inside-the-park homer—the third of that sort for the Brooks this year—and Don Demeter, . . . hit his first major league homer, also his first hit, in the eighth inning." Roscoe McGowen, *New York Times*, September 20, 1956.

Lines 45–46: *Shutting* . . . *do.* Carl Erskine's no-hitter against the Giants at Ebbets Field, May 12, 1956. *New York Times*, May 27, 1956.

Enough: Jamestown, 1607–1957 (page 16)

On May 13, 1957—the 350th anniversary of the landing at Jamestown of the first permanent English settlers in North America—three United States Air Force super sabre jets flew non-stop from London to Virginia. They were the Discovery, the Godspeed, and the Susan Constant—christened respectively by Lady Churchill, by Mrs. Whitney (wife of Ambassador John Hay Whitney), and by Mrs. W. S. Morrison (wife of the speaker of the House of Commons). *New York Times*, May 12 and 13, 1957.

The colonists entered Chesapeake Bay, having left England on New Year's Day, almost four months before, "fell upon the earth, embraced it, clutched it to them, kissed it, and, with streaming eyes, gave thanks unto God . . ." Paul Green, "The Epic of Old Jamestown," *New York Times Magazine*, March 31, 1957.

[35]

Line 54: *if present faith mend partial proof.* Dr. Charles Peabody, chaplain at Yale, 1896, author of *Mornings in College Chapel,* said past gains are not gains unless we in the present complete them.

Melchior Vulpius (*page 18*)

"And not only is the great artist mysterious to us but is that to himself. The nature of the power he feels is unknown to him, and yet he has acquired it and succeeds in directing it." Arsène Alexander, *Malvina Hoffman—Critique and Catalogue* (Paris: J. E. Pouterman, 1930).

Line 11: *Mouse-skin-bellows'-breath.* "Bird in a Bush . . . The bird flies from stem to stem while he warbles. His lungs, as in all automatons, consist of tiny bellows constructed from mouse-skin." Daniel Alain, *Réalités,* April 1957, page 58.

No better than "a withered daffodil" (*page 19*)

Line 2: "Slow, Slow, fresh Fount" by Ben Jonson, from *Cynthia's Revels*

Line 11: *a work of art.* Sir Isaac Oliver's miniature on ivory of Sir Philip Sidney. (Collection at Windsor.)

In the Public Garden (*page 20*)

Originally entitled "A Festival." Read at the Boston Arts Festival, June 15, 1958.

Lines 11–15: *Faneuil Hall . . . glittered.* "Atop Faneuil Hall, . . . market-place hall off Dock Square, Boston, Laurie Young, Wakefield gold-leafer and steeple-jack, applies . . . finishing paint on the steeple rod after . . . gilding the dome and the renowned 204-year-old grasshopper. *Christian Science Monitor,* September 20, 1946.

Line 13: *grasshopper.* "Deacon Shem Drowne's metal grasshopper, placed atop old Faneuil Hall by its creator in 1749, . . . still looks as if it could jump with the best of its kind . . . thought to be an

exact copy of the vane on top of the Royal Exchange in London."
Christian Science Monitor, February 16, 1950, quoting *Crafts of New England*, by Allen H. Eaton (New York: Harper, 1949).

Line 27: *"My work be praise."* Psalm 23—traditional Southern tune, arranged by Virgil Thomson. "President Eisenhower attributed to Clemenceau . . . the observation, 'Freedom is nothing . . . but the opportunity for self-discipline.' . . . 'And that means the work that you yourselves lay out for yourselves is worthwhile doing—doing without hope of reward.' " *New York Times*, May 6, 1958.

Saint Nicholas, (page 25)

Line 3: *a chameleon*. See photograph in *Life*, September 15, 1958, with a letter from Dr. Doris M. Cochran, curator of reptiles and amphibians, National Museum, Washington, D.C.

For February 14th (page 27)

Line 2: *"some interested law . . ."* From a poem to M. Moore by Marguerite Harris.

Combat Cultural (page 28)

Line 29: *Nan-ai-ans*. The Nanaians inhabit the frigid North of the Soviet Union.

Line 32: *one person*. Lev Golanov: "Two Boys in a Fight." Staged by Igor Moiseyev, Moiseyev Dance Company, presented in New York, 1958, by Sol Hurok.

Leonardo da Vinci's (page 30)

See *Time*, May 18, 1959, page 73: "Saint Jerome," an unfinished picture by Leonardo da Vinci, in the Vatican; and *The Belles Heures of Jean, Duke of Berry, Prince of France*, with an Introduction by James J. Rorimer (New York: Metropolitan Museum of Art, 1958).

LOYOLA COLLEGE LIBRARY